# Animal Fables
# from Aesop

ADAPTED
AND ILLUSTRATED BY

*Barbara M<u>c</u>Clintock*

David R. Godine, Publisher
Boston

FOR MY SON, LARSON

First published in 1991 by
DAVID R. GODINE, PUBLISHER, INC.
Horticultural Hall
300 Massachusetts Avenue
Boston, Massachusetts 02115

ISBN 0-87923-913-1
LC 91-55368

*Animal Fables from Aesop* was set in 13 point Adobe Garamond and
designed on the Macintosh by Caroline Hagen. Adobe Garamond
is a revival of the famous Garamond typefaces that were based on
recastings of sixteenth-century designer Claude Garamond's
original metal versions. The Adobe version was designed by
Rob Slimbach of Adobe Systems.

*First Edition*
Printed in Spain by Cayfosa, Barcelona

# The Fables

The Fox and the Crow

The Fox and the Crane

The Town Mouse and the Country Mouse

The Wolf and the Crane

The Fox and the Cat

The Wolf and the Lamb

The Crow and the Peacocks

The Fox and the Grapes

The Wolf and the Dog

The Fox        The Crane        The Cat

Allow me to introduce our cast of characters . . .

The Crows     The Lamb     The Wolf     The Mice     Assorted dogs and peacocks

## The Fox and the Crow

Out for a morning stroll, a dapper Fox spied a Crow flying overhead with a piece of cheese in her beak. He watched her as she set-
tled onto a nearby branch. "That's for me," the clever Fox  said

to himself, and walked up to the foot of the tree. "Good-day,

Mistress Crow," he cried, looking up slyly. "How well you are

looking today! How glossy your feathers; how bright

your eye! I feel certain your voice must be far sweeter

than that of other birds, just as the rest of you is

more beautiful. Please let me hear you sing

so that I may bow to you, the

Queen of Birds."

The Crow lifted her head up proudly

and began to cry, "Caw! Caw! Caw!"

But the moment she opened her mouth,

the piece of cheese fell to the ground

and was snapped up by the Fox.

"Thank you very much!" he said. "That was all
I wanted! In exchange for your cheese, I'll give you
a piece of advice—don't trust flatterers!"

## The Fox and the Crane

The Fox and the Crane were well acquainted and seemed
to enjoy each other's company.  So one day the Fox invited
his friend home for a special dinner.  For a joke, he served
nothing but some thin soup in a very shallow dish.

The Fox could easily lap
up the soup, but, no
matter how she tried,
the Crane could
only wet the
end of her long
bill in it.

"I'm sorry if the food is not to your liking," said the Fox.
The Crane was angry, but she said nothing, and left the
Fox's house as hungry as she had come.

The following day, the Fox was surprised

to receive an invitation to the

Crane's house  for lunch.

The Fox greeted the Crane graciously.  He thanked

her for the kindness of her invitation, and they

moved into the dining room.

The Crane served the meal in a long-necked jar, with an

opening so narrow the fox could only lick the outside of it.

"I won't apologize," the Crane said as she finished her

dinner. "One bad turn deserves another."

# The Town Mouse and the Country Mouse

One day a Town Mouse went to visit his cousin in the country.

This cousin was a rustic sort, but he heartily welcomed his town

kinsman. Beans and bacon, cheese and bread, were all he had

to offer, but he offered them freely.  The Town Mouse turned

up his nose at such plain fare and invited his country cousin

to visit his town home.

"Come with me and I'll show you how to live. You won't

have been in town a week before you'll wonder how you

ever could have lived in the country."

No sooner said than done: the two

mice set off.

They arrived at the Town Mouse's residence late at night.

"You'll want some refreshment after our long journey," said the

Town Mouse, and he took his cousin into the grand dining room.

There they found the remains of a fine feast, and soon the

two hungry mice were eating up jellies and cakes and all

kinds of rare delicacies.

Suddenly they heard growling and barking. "What is that?" cried the Country Mouse in alarm. "Oh, that's only the dog of the house," answered the other. "Only!" squeaked the Country Mouse. Just at that moment the door flew open and in came a huge sniffing mastiff. The two mice had to scamper off quickly and hide.

"Good-bye, cousin," said the Country Mouse, as soon

as the danger had passed.

"What! Going so soon?" asked the Town Mouse in surprise.

"Yes," the Country Mouse answered. "Better beans and

bacon in peace than cakes and ale in fear."

# The Wolf and the Crane

A Wolf was gorging on an animal he had killed, when
suddenly a small bone stuck in his throat. In terrible
pain, he ran up and down howling and groaning, trying
without success to cough up the bone. He pleaded with
everyone he met to remove it for him. "I would give
anything," he begged, "if only you would take it
out." But animal after animal refused him.

After all, who would trust a wolf?

At last the Crane took pity on the Wolf and agreed to try.

She told the Wolf to lie on his back and open his jaws

as wide as he could.

She thrust her long beak all the way down his throat.

Then she loosened the bone and pulled it out.

"Here it is," said the Crane. "Now where is the reward
you promised me?"

The Wolf grinned, showing his sharp teeth, and said: "You
should be happy. You have put your head inside a wolf's
mouth and taken it out again without harm. That ought
to be reward enough for you."

"Don't expect gratitude from the greedy," thought the Crane
to herself as she walked away.

## The Fox and the Cat

The Fox was boasting to the Cat of his cleverness in escaping
his enemies. "I have a whole bag of tricks," he said. "I know
a hundred different ways of eluding pursuit."

"I have only one," replied the Cat mildly, "but that's
enough for me."

Just at that moment they heard the cry of a pack of hounds coming toward them. The Cat immediately scampered up a tree and hid himself among the branches. "This is my method," said the Cat. "What are you going to do?"

The Fox thought first of one way, then another, then yet another. All the while the hounds came nearer and nearer.

In the end, the Fox, in his confusion, was caught by the hounds and carried away. The Cat, who had been looking on, said, "Better one sure way than a hundred you can't count on."

# The Wolf and the Lamb

One fine afternoon a Lamb was making his way down
a country road.  As he rounded a corner, a large and
hungry Wolf appeared in his path.

"You are blocking my way," bellowed the Wolf.

"But there's plenty of room for both of us,"

the Lamb replied.

"Well, then, why did you call me bad names this time
last year?" challenged the Wolf.

"That can't be," said the Lamb. "I'm only six
months old."

"Then it must have been your brother
or your sister," snarled the Wolf.
The Lamb stammered back,
"But I'm an only child."

"Then it was your father or your mother." And with

that he seized the poor Lamb and tucked him under his arm.

The Lamb managed to gasp, as he was carried away,

"Any excuse will do for a bully."

## The Crow and the Peacocks

The Crow heard that the Peacocks were having a party, and he desperately wanted to go. He knew the pretty birds would never let a plain black crow in; so he thought and thought.

Finally he decided to dress himself up in peacock feathers to fool the party-goers.

The ambitious Crow spent hours in front of his mirror, arranging and rearranging himself.

Finally, satisfied with his looks, he thought, "I'm as grand as any peacock—too grand to associate with my drab crow friends any more!" And he left his house for the party, strutting and preening the entire way.

At first all the guests were impressed by the Crow's magnificent train.

They soon discovered his disguise, however, and quickly pecked and plucked away the borrowed plumes.

The Crow, humiliated and peevish, had to return
home to all his plain crow friends, who teased him,
saying, "It's not only feathers that make fine birds."

# The Fox and the Grapes

One hot summer's day a gentleman Fox was
strolling along, when suddenly he spied a beautiful
bunch of bursting grapes hanging high on a vine
overhead.

"Just the thing to quench my thirst!"
he exclaimed.

He tried to tap them with his

walking stick, but the grapes remained

beyond his grasp.

He tried to reach them by jumping,

but still had no success.

After many attempts at jumping, he took a running leap.

He flew past the grapes . . .

. . . onto the hard, dusty ground.

At last he gave up, and walked away with his nose in the air.

He scoffed at the onlookers who had gathered, and declared,

"I never really wanted those grapes. I'm sure they're sour

anyway."

"It's easy to hate what you can't have," called a voice from those

gathered nearby.

# The Wolf and the Dog

A very thin Wolf, almost dead from hunger, went at last to visit his friend, the Dog. "Ah, friend," said the Dog, "I knew your wild life would be the ruin of you. Why don't you work steadily, like I do, and get your food given to you every day?"

"I wouldn't object," said the Wolf, "if I could only find a place."

"I could easily arrange that," said the Dog. "You can share my work guarding the house."

As the Dog reached for his pipe and tobacco, the Wolf noticed that part of the hair on the Dog's neck was worn away.

The Wolf asked how it had happened.

"Oh, it's nothing," said the Dog. "It's only the place where
my collar is put on at night to keep me chained up. It chafes
a little, but you soon get used to it."

"So that's it," said the Wolf. "Then, goodbye to you,
Master Dog. It's better to starve free than be a fat slave."

*And so ends our Animal Aesops!*